THE
DARK

BY

LEMONY SNICKET

ILLUSTRATED BY

JON KLASSEN

ORCHARD

Laszlo was
afraid of
the dark.

The dark lived in the same
house as Laszlo,
a big place with a creaky roof,
smooth, cold windows
and several flights of stairs.

Sometimes
the dark hid
in the cupboard.

Sometimes
it sat behind
the shower curtain.

But mostly it spent its
time in the basement.
All day long the dark would
wait in a distant corner, far
from the squeaks and rattles
of the washing machine,
pressed up against some old,
damp boxes and a chest of
drawers nobody ever opened.

At night, of course, the dark
went out and spread itself
against the windows
and doors of
Laszlo's house.

But in the morning
the dark would be
back in the basement,
where it belonged.
Laszlo would peek at the
dark every morning.

"Hi,"
he would say.
"Hi, dark."

Laszlo thought that
if he visited the dark
in the dark's room,
maybe the dark
wouldn't come and
visit him in his room.

But one night –

it did.

"Laszlo," the dark said,
in the dark.

The voice of the dark was as creaky
as the roof of the house, and as smooth and
cold as the windows, and even though the dark
was right next to Laszlo, the
voice seemed very far away.

"What do
you want?"
asked Laszlo.

"I want to
show you
something,"
said the dark.

"Yes," said the dark.

In Laszlo's living room was
the biggest window
in the house.
Laszlo looked out at all the
dark outside. Above him
the roof creaked, and he
closed his eyes. Now the
dark was all Laszlo could see.

"No, no," said the dark again.
"Not there."

"In the basement?" asked Laszlo.

"Yes," said the dark.

Laszlo had never dared come to the dark's room at night.

"Come closer," said the dark.

Laszlo came closer.

"Even closer,"
said the dark.

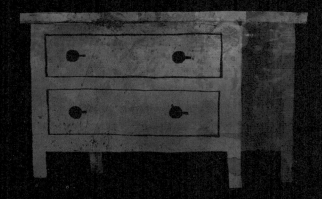

You might be afraid of the dark, but the dark is not afraid of you. That's why the dark is always close by.

The dark peeks round the corner and waits behind the door, and you can see the dark up in the sky almost every night, gazing down at you as you gaze up at the stars.

Without a creaky roof, the rain would fall on your bed, and without a smooth, cold window, you could never see outside, and without a flight of stairs, you could never go into the basement, where the dark spends its time.

Without a cupboard, you would have nowhere to put your shoes, and without a shower curtain, you would splash water all over the bathroom, and without the dark, everything would be light, and you would never know if you needed a lightbulb.

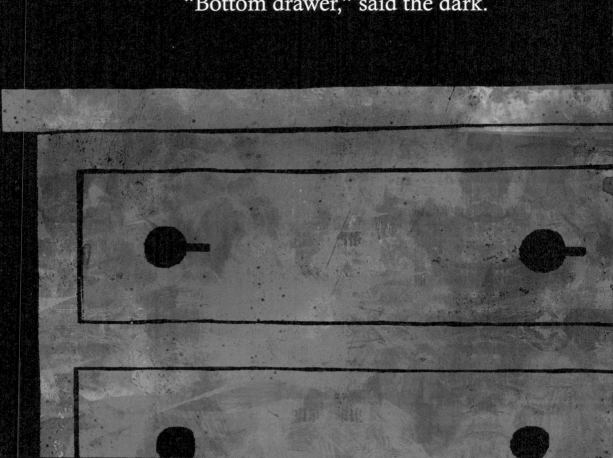

"Bottom drawer," said the dark.

"What?"

"Bottom drawer,"
said the dark.
"Open the bottom
drawer."

"Thank you,"
said Laszlo.

"You're
welcome,"
said the dark.

By the time Laszlo got back into bed,

the dark was no longer in his room,

except when he closed his eyes to go to sleep.

The next morning, Laszlo visited the dark in the basement.

"Hi," he said.
"Hi, dark."

The dark didn't answer,
but the bottom
drawer was still
open, so it looked
like something in the
corner was smiling.

The dark kept
on living with
Laszlo, but it
never bothered
him again.

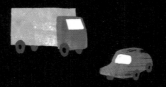

LEMONY SNICKET has been accused of leaving his readers in the dark. He is the author of numerous bestselling books, including those in A Series of Unfortunate Events and All the Wrong Questions. You can learn more at www.LemonySnicketLibrary.com.

JON KLASSEN was born in Winnipeg, USA, where the dark arrives early for much of the year. He has written and illustrated many books, including *I Want My Hat Back* and *This is Not My Hat*. You can see more of his work at www.beastofburden.com.

ORCHARD BOOKS 338 Euston Road, London NW1 3BH • *Orchard Books Australia* Level 17/207 Kent Street, Sydney, NSW 2000 • First published in 2013 in the United States by Little, Brown and Company • This edition published by Orchard Books in 2013 Text © Lemony Snicket 2013 • Illustrations © Jon Klassen 2013 • Cover illustrations © 2013 by Jon Klassen • Cover design © 2013 Hachette Book Group, Inc. The rights of Lemony Snicket to be identified as the author and of Jon Klassen to be identified as the illustrator of this work have been asserted by them in accordance with the Copyright, Designs and Patents Act, 1988 • A CIP catalogue record for this book is available from the British Library • ISBN 978 1 40833 002 9 • 10 9 8 7 6 5 4 3 2 1 • Printed in China • Orchard Books is a division of Hachette Children's Books, an Hachette UK company • www.hachette.co.uk